To,
Stuart

Signed by Zagham Karim

14-08-16

About the Author:

Zagham was born on the 23rd of July 1998. His early childhood was spent in a town called Dudley, where he spent most of his free times in reading fictional novels.

After which he moved to Pakistan. He spent his early teens there, attending Hira School in Bewal and later moving to The City School, Islamabad- where he completed his O'Levels. It was books like 'A Tale of Two Cities' and a collection of short stories that were part of the syllabus which interested him to write his own novels. Which others could enjoy, just like he enjoyed reading through a good novel.

He began to write various short stories in school. Now he has begun to make use of some of the ideas from those short stories; by writing novels in his free time. Most of his work is set in the sci-fi/fantasy genre.

His first novella is called 'Town of Dudley Sixth' and is about an apocalypse on an alien planet. Some aspects of the novella are inspired by his interest in mechanical timepieces.

Especially ones that include the tourbillon and minute repeater function with skeletal design.

For example, the use of mechanical technology in transport, gates and timekeeping. Other aspects are inspired by his interest in aeronautical/aerospace engineering- such as the spaceship.

TOWN OF DUDLEY SIXTH

About the Author:

In short, his novels are a means of expressing his emotion and in some ways, various concepts are understandable as they apply to us humans as well- such as infrastructure of buildings and the ranking system.

Introduction

He was alone as he hovered above the town hall, in the last moments of the day. Despite the fact it was in a city, the residents still called it the town hall. The very words had been engraved into the building. It could be that he chose the town hall as it was close to the centre of Lukemilldale, even though the city had an irregular shape. The streets were now silent, the only indication that it was night— other than a general guess based on the time of the day.

Fate, had cast a spell of everlasting darkness. Dark clouds filled the sky, preventing even a single ray of light, from touching the surface. The clouds never moved nor did it rain. Not many remembered the giant orb of light that had once heated the planet.

Since the day the collision occurred, darkness had enveloped the planet. As a direct result, the atmosphere had broken down and a thick layer of dusty clouds had formed in the skies, which were held in place by frozen gases. This had also led to the crumbling of the space defence system, allowing aliens to enter without anyone noticing. The defence system consisted of the celestial objects around the planet and watch towers, which had been demolished by the collision.

The day after the collision, only one city was found to be unaffected by the catastrophe. The situation went from bad to worse. Everything changed that day; either you were the predator or the prey. Survivors divided into two factions: those inside the city walls and those outside its protection. There was little effort to rebuild cities across the planet compared to the effort being put into

TOWN OF DUDLEY SIXTH

leaving the planet. Some people began to tell the year relative to the collision, due to the catastrophic effect it had. Even those within the city's walls no longer valued the luxury of residing in Lukemilldale. A city modernised by Dudley (sixth duke of planet Kepler), especially now that the currency no longer held value nor did luxury assure normality.

Chapter 0

The Collision

Moreover, the collision was no ordinary feat, as the colliding object was a ghost spacecraft. Perhaps it was scary enough that it crash-landed into a planet protected by other celestial bodies around it, but even more mysterious and creepy was how the spacecraft became a ghost spacecraft. Twenty-three years after the collision, the memory was still fresh in the mind of the man who hovered over a certain building and scanned the streets for any suspicious activity, but found nothing abnormal. Bored from the lack of activity, he drifted into a state of thought.

Pondering about the fate of his race, the figure tightened his grip on an ornament, something found outside the city soon after the collision. Deeply engraved into the ornament were the words 'Half Guilloche'. Somehow these plain words felt like the key to a hidden meaning, a meaning much more significant than the collision itself.

Unfortunately, at the moment there were more important issues to handle, such as the scarcity of food and other vital resources. More survivors were sent to patrol the outside world, further from the wall to scavenge for resources. Water was something the survivors had learnt to create artificially, yet little progress was made on a sustainable food supply. Scavengers also brought back parts of the spacecraft, especially the more experienced units that ventured further from the city walls into enemy territory. Not all of

TOWN OF DUDLEY SIXTH

them returned; however, the survivors were desperate with time running against them.

Ironically, the cause of all the destruction was the only hope of survival. Parts of the spacecraft that were brought back were inspected by engineers so they could use the knowledge acquired from those parts to build another spacecraft. It would prove to be a difficult task, due to the fact that no one on the planet was a spacecraft engineer. Considering how this was the largest spacecraft they had ever seen. Making one would be no stroll in the park.

On the other hand, the question that everyone avoided thinking or even talking about was how long the city would hold out. Beyond the wall was a world full of danger and death, the difference between both sides was so great they could have been living in different dimensions. Hence, beyond the safety of the city walls the world was named 'Tenebris Mundo', meaning the darkened world.

Tenebris Mundo consisted of rogue survivors, who were cannibals. To hunt, they had somewhat of a council, which also ensured that they hunted only within their designated areas. Their leadership resulted in organised attempts to break into the city walls, but none of their attempts succeeded- as the walls were made from strong and rare metals extracted from meteoroids. Not to mention they were led by a fanatic ruler who was by far the most barbaric of all rogue survivors, as he made slaves of even the mutants, they were the individuals who were close to the site of impact and due to the spread of toxic gases and chemicals from the spacecraft had evolved.

TOWN OF DUDLEY SIXTH

Consequently, Lukemilldale, a once proud twelve-lettered city, marched toward its doom, not that the twelve letters made a difference now. Considering that the ranking system of the galaxy, according to which the luxury and security of a city was ranked with the number of letters in the name, was no longer valid seeing how the planet was cut off from its neighbours. All these thoughts raced through the mind of the figure that hovered as a high ranking officer who ranked far above the rookie amateurs, being the head commander of the legendary warriors.

The wounds of the past now hurt more than ever, as it seemed that the inevitable annihilation of the alien race was inevitable. Just as he thought that- he saw smoke in the distance, far from the walls boundary as if it was a camp fire. It looked as it came from over the horizon. Then more and more camp fires were lit; it seemed the enemy had made their move. As he hovered in the air, watching the city like a guardian angel, he thought of a plan to counter the attack, but for that he would need reinforcements.

Meanwhile, an alien scurried along the dusty streets, ignorant of the cool breeze that would have chilled most life forms to the bone. It moved without precaution or fear; either it did not hear the terrifying sounds of bloodthirsty predators awaiting their prey or it pretended not to. His thunderous footsteps echoed through the empty streets.

If not for the alien, there would have been a petrifying silence. It was astonishing that a being, dwarfed in comparison to its surrounding structures, made such sounds. With a height of fifty-seven inches, the alien was not tall. Therefore, it was not very daunting in

TOWN OF DUDLEY SIXTH

appearance. However, the alien was not to be underestimated. In the dim light of the glowing street lamps, an outline to the alien could be seen as it robotically walk-jogged down the streets.

The light revealed perfectly round, ruby eyes shimmering through the dark, an even more prominent feature than the curved cheekbones that made it look tough. Its eyes bode well in the shade of thick silver eyebrows, which melted into its metallic skin, as they sat above a sharp nose. The supersonic funnels on the sides of its head, or perhaps a mouth that seemed to be carved by a shallow tool made it alien, but the emerald mountainous hair was what made it look divine, as if it were a mythical creature straight out of a book.

The alien was draped in dark robes of animal skin decorated with light patterns in silk. On its right arm, the alien wore the sixth form emblem, above the embroidery of his given masculine name 'Sambol'. On its feet it wore rubber shoes, designed to fit all without variation.

Sambol's only companion was the slab of metal and gears on his wrist, with hand-engraved patterns on the skeleton dial, boasting seven gongs and a silvery white case holding all the working parts together. Unfortunately, it had betrayed him by reading fifteen minutes to nine and it would take him ten to get home. This would cause problems between him and his mother, since she strictly asked him to be home by thirty minutes past eight as lunch would be at nine. On top of the scolding he would not get any dinner, unless he got there in the next five minutes, spent five apologising, and then used the rest getting ready for dinner.

TOWN OF DUDLEY SIXTH

The Collision

Sambol's mother, Moranta, maintained strict expectations with regard to time management, cleanliness, and honesty. Added to the shortages in food, which mandated rationing- allowing for only two meals a day. As the barren land held no hope for rehabilitation, the situation was becoming more and more hopeless.

But it sure seemed like Sambol's lucky day today. Steps away was his house, two decades ago it was priceless, now it was worthless except for its shelter. His heartbeat reached a climatic pulse and his breath got heavier with each step. Each second ticked by, as time momentarily stopped when he passed someone draped in a cloak. The stranger had a dark aura reflective of an ill omen, but Sambol did not have time to investigate. Ignoring the encounter, he barged in through the welcoming front door of a house, which looked like every other house on the street from outside, locked all thirty-six bolts and engaged the seventy-four locks locking system. It seemed he was the last to reach home. He always enjoyed watching the locks click into place as the gears rotated continuously, but at that moment, time was of the essence.

Unconsciously, Sambol beamed at his handicraft before he snapped back to his senses, realising he was late. Out of nowhere, his mother appeared and began her lecture.

Knowing something was wrong from her expressions, Sambol expected a drastic change in his lifestyle. Whilst father waited for his dinner, he began to fidget with his newspaper before deciding to read it. Today mother did not scold the meek man hiding behind the sheets of newspaper for not taking family time seriously. Something was definitely fishy. Even though

TOWN OF DUDLEY SIXTH

the more Sambol tried to avoid being the centre of attention, fate worked against his cause.

Chapter 1
The Family Meeting

"In a world of eternal slumber,
it is but wise to foresee the future.

Where true beauty is priceless,
for creativity can be so far ahead.

Do our eyes not see that far ahead,
does our brain make baseless theories in greed?

Here we live in a world of zombies,
value is only for the present, who cares about the future?

Our air is cold and bitter, the sky is ever dark,
and the land is barren, for the earth is in parts.

Long ago, it was not when began the curse,
in a time when all was but lost.

Tall buildings seared through the dark clouds,
but no height made visible even a ray of light.

A city built in ruins and curses,
never is it filled with zeal and happiness.

People however, can choose to defy nature,
jewels of ruby and stones of blue sapphire.

All were embedded in layers of white gold,
the gold that coated the mechanised bricks.

TOWN OF DUDLEY SIXTH

The Family Meeting

Bricks of steel and skeleton design,
they shifted forever each year with a chime.

Sound of cogs, when metal contacted metal,
made lively the mood of a silent city.

Grey were the streets and white were the roads
street lamps of rose gold, enclosing bulbs of diamond pose.

Diamonds that were alien used to trap small stars,
forever emitting a bright white light.

Fake flowers of caesium behind gates of rubidium,
were held in place with emerald stems.

Each building unique and everything but bleak,
with engraved patterns of blue platinum nailed into walls.

Gold roofs and doors with all their glory,
windows of minerals and tampered glass.

A beauty it was and a shame to be true,
each night when the lockdown began.

Barriers were raised and gates were closed,
doors and windows were securely locked.

Curtains drawn and lights switched off,
lamps were covered as the dark night dragged on....."

TOWN OF DUDLEY SIXTH

The Family Meeting

I was told history repeats itself, so does that mean we are going around in circles, or are we spiralling into darkness?

Around a polished wooden table, a family enjoyed a dinner they deserved. With the exception of the middle-son, who had nothing to enjoy in the first place. His family was a happy one, a small community in itself. It consisted of six members who now sat around a rectangular dining table, with the father at the short end.

Their house was quite exquisite, as it dripped with chandeliers; holding multiple orbs of light. Lavish carpets cushioned the floor with twists of: red, blue and gold. Guilloche patterns drilled into the pale yellow roof and wallpapers gilded the silver walls. The front door led to the main hall- from which the kitchen, sitting room, dining room and drawing room opened. As such each member of the family valued the privacy of his or her own room.

Back at the table, Sambol was troubled by the numerous glances directed at him in the midst of a dinner, where no one uttered a single word. He was thought of as simple minded and lazy. But he was really quite the opposite, a bright person who was very creative. This was reflected in his tasks and hobby as a watchmaker.

Normally, Sambol would eat his share of burnt leaves on roasted twigs, slowly, so as to fully enjoy the taste. Especially with less food to eat there was no point in rushing through meals. The glass of water that went with the meal was usually refreshing- despite being artificially produced. But not today, he was in philosophical thought when he heard a faint thud sound

TOWN OF DUDLEY SIXTH

in the distance. But as no one else in the room appeared to hear it, so he ignored it with the thought that he had imagined it.

Soon after everyone finished their meal, father (Grumlov- pronounced with the 'v' silent) began the family discussion, "I know things have been rough on you. Since our resources have been dwindling- so has our activity. There is no longer school, college or much recreational work. But the situation is going to get worse, as we now have more incursions occurring; our walls are not going to protect us forever. The head council has decided to take action based upon the mayors' advice." Stated Grumlov, then after a slight pause he continued on to say, "They want to recruit more personnel for the defence and scavenging departments. You see, as a father, I cannot bear to see any one of you to be chosen. I hope you understand."

Sambol's little brother Lazlo interrupted, "But father, it is our duty to contribute, as we owe this city for keeping us alive for so long. This is our responsibility as citizens. We can't just hide, when things get a little tough; hoping for things to fix themselves."

Lazlo's older brother- Arantus, backed him up, "I agree, as we all know the punishment for cheating the authority: exile into the outside world. I don't want to live thinking that every breath could be my last. If I'm going to be anywhere, it's on this side of the wall."

"I can see what your point is, but look at things from my perspective. You are my children, I love you, and I can't bear to lose you. Not knowing if you are dead or alive, not being able to see you until your year of service comes to an end. Only for you, to be sent back when the next rotation begins. Look, I am simply stating my opinion based on my life experiences, the decision is in your hands." Replied a solemn Grumlov.

Sambol was dumbfounded, he knew Grumlov to be a strong man, but today he melted before his kin. Just imagining what kind of horrors could be out there, horrors that disturbed his father so deeply that he didn't want his children to share the same fate. It gave Sambol cold chills, he couldn't just be his rebellious self and say, "We will do what we must for the wellbeing of the city. All those people working hard to keep us citizens alive; they deserve our respect." Instead he respected his father with silence.

Seeing how the table was surrounded by sorrow and tension- as the next person to speak, would steer the conversation and be responsible for the consequences. Mother was the only one capable of breaking the tense silence, so she stepped into the conversation. "I think that is enough talk for one day- go get some rest now dear. As for the rest of you, Engelia can come help me do the dishes while the rest of you should head back to your rooms."

With that father made his way upstairs, soon after which Sambol left for his room, dragging his feet- mostly because he was working with an empty stomach. Engelia (Sambol's older sister) then went into the kitchen to help mother do her chores, while Lazlo and Arantus also headed to their rooms.

In his room, Sambol was thinking about the 'family talk'. Despite being short, it had managed to cast a thick blanket of despair on the house, pushing everyone

TOWN OF DUDLEY SIXTH

between a rock and a hard place. So as to divert his attention from the events of the day, he unpacked his watch making equipment and set to work.

Of course, he could never be as good as Eric- a family friend and neighbour. He was the one who taught Sambol watch making. Eric was a prestige master horologer who worked to make timepieces for the soldiers. Mostly he focused on making precise timepieces, focusing on the accuracy. But rarely did he spend time on making something innovative. He wasn't thought of well by all high ranking individuals- just an extra mouth to feed.

However, he was not bothered in the least. He was proud of his work, as at the pinnacle of haute horology, was his masterpiece. A wrist watch that utilised a complex movement, it compromised of two hundred and eighty jewels alongside one hundred and eighty eight ball bearings. It also had eleven gongs; being a decimal minute repeater and grand sonnerie. The gongs also acted as an alarm function, to wake him up in the morning. Seven mini barrels provided a power reserve of one hundred and thirty hours, with one barrel dedicated to three tourbillons. The entire mechanism was visible on the dial and through the case back, with black diamond's set on gold poudre to represent the hour markers. Its case was decorated with waves of: black, silver and white intertwined together, bound to the wrist by an elegant leather strap.

TOWN OF DUDLEY SIXTH

Chapter 2
A Hidden Truth

Engelia had a bronze complexion, which bode well with her round face. Her eyes oscillated between orange and red based on her emotions, it was what made her different. She usually kept her burgundy hair tidy, nicely tied up. But today she had them all curled up, resting on her shoulder. In terms of height she was three inches taller than Sambol, but never really cared.

She was the type of person that thought about others, being the responsible one in the family. Today she wore a purple dress, with dark green heels- as the colour helped clear her mind. Being a kind hearted person with a strong sense of justice, meant that she always had to do the right thing.

The notice from the council didn't help ease things. It stated that the legendary knights would come around the city in order of the sectors. They would be selecting new soldiers for the defence and scavenging departments, although they would have to take part in the entrance test before being recruited. As such the four siblings had decided to use a weapon they specialised in, so if by chance or for some reason they were chosen for the test. They could decide the outcome.

Being residents of the city meant they had to start self-defence training at an early age. The training included choosing a weapon to master alongside hand to hand combat. However, Sambol was forced to choose an

TOWN OF DUDLEY SIXTH

additional weapon; due to the lack of ammo for his handgun, so he picked a sword.

To prevent Sambol from seeing himself as alienated, the others also picked two weapons. Arantus used a staff that could be converted into a spear; he also had globes of chemical explosives. Engelia used a bow and arrow paired with a battle axe, while Lazlo used a resonating hammer alongside his set of poisoned knifes. His resonating hammer was made from a material that constantly resonated and was hard to control, but it certainly packed a punch.

Back inside a cosy mansion, Sambol's heart was divided; he was perplexed whether to follow his father's will or try to achieve a destiny greater than what his father had in mind for him. But his father was no longer the man he used to be. These days Grumlov no longer drove a car or was as spirited in mechanical technology. He once enjoyed charging the engine by turning its handle. He was mesmerised by the moving gears which displayed when the number plate window was removed. Ever since he had spent his year of service in the defence department, things had changed. Grumlov no longer had an interest in mechanical technology and grew distant from his family. Being the one closest to his father, Sambol embraced his interests as his own, which ironically-rubbed on their relation.

At the moment, Sambol decided he could use some fresh air, so he went out for a walk. He walked through Silverwosh Park, a place he often visited since childhood. He wondered about the park's history before the collision. Greenery, a rush of people enjoying themselves, and the rides danced through his mind. (Unfortunately,

TOWN OF DUDLEY SIXTH

the rides were scrapped away, to be used as 'essential resources').

He looked at the ruined city, contemplating his decision. Pondering how his actions would affect others. When he couldn't think any longer, he went back home. Upon reaching his house, he took a deep breath and stepped in; expecting a confrontation with his father- as he was rebellious and father spent a lot of time convincing him to do things his way. However, he did not hear the normal rumble of voices. Instead, he heard nothing until he moved closer to the stairs. His father and mother were debating in whispers. Usually, he ignored them, but that day he wanted to hear what they were talking about.

He could not hear clearly but he heard mother say "I think it's about time.... the right to know"

So he stepped a few steps closer to the drawing room, until he was standing just outside the room. Only to hear Grumlov say"... Besides, I don't want to talk about this now, we'll talk later. You never know who could be listening," in a sharp tone, causing Sambol to take a few steps out of view.

To which Moranta cut in and said, "When is it going to be the right time? We both know that 'later' never comes to pass, so I will tell him if you can't, he should know if he is chosen."

Ending the conversation, Grumlov said, "I know how much he cares for me, the knights only take recruits who show potential. If he doesn't show any he won't be picked, even if he does he will not make it through the entrance test."

TOWN OF DUDLEY SIXTH

To which mother sighed and replied, "Okay, but we will have to tell him at some point. I hope you understand that we can't keep it a secret forever."

After which she came out the room and headed to the kitchen to make lunch, failing to see Sambol hurriedly hide behind a bunch of flower pots. At least today, he had nothing bad to say about the decorative ornaments mother had put around the house; even fake flowers were beautiful in their own way.

Sambol stayed there long after father headed upstairs- probably to wake everyone up. He stayed- so as to avoid his parent's sharp eyes and ears. After which he went back to the front door, walking back into the hall. He now headed for the sitting room, engaging himself in a story book while sitting on the couch. He wanted to forget everything he had just heard, but the thought of his parents keeping a secret bugged him. It disturbed him, for whatever they were hiding it had to be serious.

Finally, lunch was served and he acted like nothing had happened at all. Engelia did ask if he was feeling well, but no one else really said anything else. So the day passed, even in the evening he couldn't concentrate on his watch making, with so much going on. Boredom ate at him, so he ended up going to sleep early today.

That night he had very weird dreams. He saw aliens that called themselves humans. They fought each other for trivial reasons with dangerous weapons. They had fast cars which ran on 'electricity' and natural resources.

That mysterious 'electricity' was used in all kinds of things. They made metal birds called planes which were used for travelling. Such weird dreams they were,

Sambol found the idea amusing because everything was mechanical, and had to be charged to store energy.

His dreams took a sharp turn. He imagined he was one of the humans- that he was far from home. He wanted to be return to his parents, for he did not care about the circumstances as long as his friends and family were with him. But this dream was only the beginning of his many haunting nightmares.

TOWN OF DUDLEY SIXTH

Chapter 3
Recruitment at Last

On the day the knights were to come; to select recruits for the entrance exam, everyone stood outside their houses in a straight line waiting for their arrival. The air resonated with vibes of anxiety. Sambol still felt confused and wondered would if his father would be happy or ashamed if he wasn't even considered or a bit of both?

Trying to distract himself, Sambol thought of strategies to use. So as to not be demeaned, but somehow still please his father; but he couldn't think of anything else. His pride was important and so was his father. After all he had decided to live his father's dream, but what could he do now. He was in quite the pickle. He did all he could in hoping that something good would happen, whatever the outcome was, whilst he waited.

Waiting, was cruel, his heart skipped a beat every time he heard a sound approaching. It took a while for the distant sound of hooves to become audible. The sound became louder, until a trail of dust was visible a few blocks down the street. The dust didn't make the knights happy, after all the cleaners had taken a day off because of them, but it served to foul their mood a little. It must have been rough on them, working while everyone else had a day off.

A few of them slowed their horses, while the rest continued on. It would have been nice to see actual ones, considering these were genetically modified clones.

One of the knights seemed to be in his fifties, perhaps he had volunteered to work for the defence department. He still looked fit and daunting, even his scars made him look tough. He would be a challenging foe in battle. The other knight was in his twenties and looked much tougher, even though he was younger; he seemed superior in rank.

It seemed like it took all day for a knight to make it to Sambol's house. The one evaluating them was the older knight. He looked over Sambol and his brothers and spoke in a sharp tone, "My name is Jiva. It seems you are all well-equipped- quite a variety of weapons you all have. You look like the eldest son, what is your name boy?"

"Sire, I am Arantus. But I am not that well trained."

Jiva thought about it for a second, and then answered, "Well we can train you, as long as you can learn. Who is that standing next to you?"

"Sir, I am Sambol"

"Splendid. Both of you come tomorrow to the local green belt, I think in this area, you call it Silverwosh park. Oh, you are going to have to go there and present them this paper to enrol." said Jiva, handing them an enrolment letter.

He turned to leave, but then stopped. Grumlov's heart began to race. Jiva waved his finger and said, "I almost forgot to do the scavenging departments recruitment. You there, you look as if you'd do well, what is your name?"

A dazzled Engelia blurted, "Mister Jiva, my name is Engelia."

To which he laughed, saying "Well, you should go to the green belt too. The entrance tests for both departments will be taking place next week. I'd advise some practice."

TOWN OF DUDLEY SIXTH

Recruitment at Last

Grumlov walked silently into the house, while the knight proceeded to the next house. It was his way, of letting his offspring know that he wanted them to decide their own future; although it was evident he wanted them to stay home, he left the choice in their capable hands. Sambol had thoughts otherwise- he had always looked up to the knights, with the light armour they wore. They continued to surprise Sambol. He had expected them to wear sturdy armour; instead they wore something so light. It came to show how brave they were. When they walked, it was with an aura of confidence and caution. Those were just the tip of the iceberg for the abilities they had, which was why he wanted to be like them.

Sambol hoped the days would whiz by until the test, but he definitely didn't expect them to. His siblings mostly stayed out of touch, busy training themselves or spending some alone time. Sambol was not in the least bothered. Perhaps they could not see the world the way he could. Thinking about it didn't change anything, so he slept knowing it might be the last time his whole family slept under this roof, at least until their year of service ended.

On the day of the test, the selected recruits were herded to Silverwosh Park. It was one of many tests occurring across the city. The vacant space served as a great spot to remind the selected few why they were there. Lazlo, Arantus and Sambol stood in a corner at the open side of the park, while Engelia stood on the other side waiting for her turn, among the tree stumps rotting away in the cold. The parents of all the candidates waited at the entrance of the park.

Talking was prohibited as the entrance test commenced. The knights tested first the more muscular candidates who looked as though they would do well. However, not all of them did as well as they were

TOWN OF DUDLEY SIXTH

expected to do. In the first phase, which was about long range combat- around half the candidates had already been eliminated. Sambol could see that some of them purposefully underperformed, however they weren't punished. Sambol did see someone write something down, every time someone underperformed. But they could not just kick them and their families all out into Tenebris Mundo. It would greatly reduce the community size; after all they were either cowards or just not bothered about things. Some were in the same position as him, under family pressure- but at a more extreme level. He was not one to judge, so he stood still, silently watching.

Among the last few to be tested were Sambol and his siblings. When it was his turn, Sambol became excited to use his gun to show off his skills. He aimed at the furthest target, at a distance meant for long range bows or sniper rifles. He remained focused; his gun was aimed at the goal, when he steadily pulled the trigger.

Some people would have closed their eye, but he kept them open and watched the bullet hit the exact centre. The surrounding onlookers were shocked and the officers showed dismay. Despite his age, he was well experienced with a howitzer hand gun, which most people did not use due to its recoil. Many individuals could not shoot a bullet close to the goal, even with years of experience. Yet, Sambol had mastered the weapon.

After a slight pause, the audience applauded him while other competitors were a mix of beams and scorns. Modestly, he walked to the side, where he was told he would be participating in the second phase. Arantus was the next contestant. He used his staff as a spear. Tension oozed through his demeanour. Then he threw it with his full strength, to his own dismay he had missed his target by a few yards. It had been an honest throw, maybe he had cramped his muscles due to the excessive training he had done to get used to it again.

Since he had not performed at a good enough level, they overlooked him. This caused Sambol to ponder, how come they weren't choosing people that could be taught to improve? It was almost as if they were choosing people just before a war. But he could be over thinking.

TOWN OF DUDLEY SIXTH

Chapter 4
Saying Goodbye

The test for the scavenging department was picking at least three useful materials from among the tree trumps in three minutes, then state the use of the materials as to what it could be used for. A maximum of ten objects could be taken. The exam grew difficult for the testers selected last, however their points increased for finding a material. It was finally Engelia's turn, but she was struggling. In the first two minutes, she had found only one useful material. With only a minute to go, it seemed she would not be selected.

Moranta saw the mocking looks of the people when they watched Engelia perform. Secretly, she wished for her to perform well and to be chosen. She hoped her children would return honourably, to show all the original residents that they weren't better or superior to the survivors. With only forty seconds to spare, Engelia had found her second item. The examiners began to laugh at her among themselves, when only twenty seconds remained. A few seconds later she saw an item a little burrowed in the ground, she could risk looking at what it was or just look around elsewhere. She took the risk, which was worth it, as with only three seconds left she had got all three items. With a half-hearted smile, the examiners had passed her.

Then the second phase of the defence department began. The theme was close range combat. In this part, candidates were paired to fight against each other, in a 'disciplined manner'. The fights were to be fair, where

TOWN OF DUDLEY SIXTH

marks would be awarded on general performance rather than the result of the fight.

Ironically, the close range combat was more fruitful than the first phase. Sambol was among the first few to be selected as he did well against his opponent, using his momentum against him. His swordsmanship was tested next, as he was pitted against a few dummy targets. Which he easily sliced through, demolishing them all within a few seconds, as if they were made of paper. His performance showed his sharp muscle reflexes, which got him extra points. On the whole he was one of the above average recruits.

The event soon ended, with seven selected for the defence department and thirteen for the scavenging department, from the original forty-six. An announcement was made that a carriage departing for the training ground would be waiting for them the next day- sharp at seven in the morning. Following the announcement, the knights left.

Father didn't converse much with them during the day, as he respected their decision, but at the same time wished he could undo it. Sambol packed his trunk, he placed his half made watch and a few smaller watch making tools inside, along with his clothes. Meanwhile, Moranta helped Engelia in her packing, talking about how she would pray for her wellbeing whenever she missed her. She advised Engelia to follow her destiny, to forge her own path.

Meanwhile, Sambol went to Eric's place to bid him farewell. They talked about watches, about the different designs they were hoping to incorporate into their next

TOWN OF DUDLEY SIXTH

watches. It was their way of communicating. Seeing how Eric was like a teacher and role model to Sambol. He was keen to learn new things from Eric. Today Eric wished him good luck, as they greeted each other good bye.

Early next morning they got ready to leave. Grumlov spoke to the both of them saying how he would remember them, while they were away. He advised Sambol to be extra careful and told Engelia, "I'm sure you will be fine at the Eastern border, there aren't many skirmishes on that side. But you are to be careful out there."

When the carriages arrived, Sambol and Engelia said goodbye to each other and went their separate ways.

TOWN OF DUDLEY SIXTH

Chapter 5
Ride through the City

Sambol expected the carriage which bore the recruits, to be cramped and reek of pungent smells. Pleasantly surprised, he had enough room to sit comfortably and no putrid smells lingered in the vehicle. Sambol recalled the rumours that the spacecraft was near completion. It seemed the city officials wanted to maximise its defences, by fully utilising their resources. Considering how spacious the vehicle was, he realised this would be the final push.

Sitting by the window, gave him a good view of the city. He had never really come far from his house, as he knew it would be the same everywhere. These days, he saw more buildings than he saw people. The buildings reached for the sky, but fell short in comparison to the clouds. How the sky mocked them all with its height, it was just beyond their reach. But that was sure to change, hopefully sometime soon.

Stained by dark clouds, the sky extinguished the warm rays of the giant orb. As the battle between the elements of nature raged on, the rookies made their way to camp. Memories of his younger brother visited Sambol. They were often mistaken as twins, if not for the height difference and Lazlo's hazelnut brown eyes, they might as well have been.

Sambol would miss him, a lot more than he would miss Arantus. Arantus was the one who looked a lot more like father. Father had a muscular figure, despite having a

TOWN OF DUDLEY SIXTH

short height. He was still five/six inches taller than Sambol. But compared to the average height of the residents, which was seven feet, he was really short. Grumlov kept his white hair short, mostly because it looked good on his grey skin. His eyes were dark- pitch black. Which made him look emotionless, but he was by no means emotionless. His beard was what gave him character. He was the only one with a beard in the family- excluding Arantus.

Arantus was the tallest in the family. His height was six foot eight inches. Unlike Lazlo, who was a bit chubby, Arantus was well built. But his turquoise hair was never one size; he hated having a haircut, so he had it very short. Only for it to grow long again and regretfully be demolished yet again. It was his one downside, other than his distinctive hyena laugh. Added to his yellow/gold skin and purple eyes, his beard made him look serious and cool. But he was not even close to serious- being the funny guy who cracked jokes and pulled pranks at others expense.

Back in the carriage, Sambol observed the other rookies as they neared camp. Some of them were cowards with fear painted on their face. Others were brave warriors with a sense of purpose and pride. The recruit sitting next to Sambol looked more determined than all the others.

He was a few inches taller than Sambol; dressed in funky clothes which suited his circular physique. His short grey hair was well shaped. But his square nose clashed with his sea green, triangular eyes, which rested under his thin, magenta eyebrows. Sambol got his name, during his conversation with the other recruits, as 'Zain'.

TOWN OF DUDLEY SIXTH

It seemed he preferred to talk to those who were realistic and brave like himself. Sambol would definitely proof himself worthy friendship. Zain's confidence had inspired Sambol. Perhaps with him around the camp would not be that bad after all, not as bad as father had told him.

With that the caravan finally entered the camp. Everyone stepped out gladly to stretch their legs and get some rest. But the site before them chilled them to their bone.

TOWN OF DUDLEY SIXTH

Chapter 6
Trained to be Warriors

"The path to destiny being so wonderful in nature,
so few dare to take its path so freely.

It gives life a unique structure,
indeed a true image of you it displays.

In a plain which seems to have no bound,
how far can the path before you be?

Life is not long enough to see it all;
only a few steps it can give.

So should one then cower in fear?
Or with chivalry and honour take the steps.

Lest not many live to see their desires fulfil,
can you do what they all could not?

Your heart can only show the path,
will you take it now or when you no longer live?

What of those who came before you?
Surely they must have walked a long way.

Mighty souls band not far from here,
life they value but not their own.

Hope is something that will always be,
but in this world of delusion it cannot stay.

TOWN OF DUDLEY SIXTH

Trained to be Warriors

A band of warrior's joins to defend us all,
together they are a mighty force.

Now they train together, for a mighty cause,
a building there is for each group and rank.

Tall buildings there are twenty three;
all have domed doors through which sounds a great roar.

Square windows are for the highly proud,
below which the training ground holds a crowd.

Some come while some go,
in a building graced with precious stone.

Here they stay in a small cramped room,
training to fight their impending doom.

Eat they do in a barn full of heat;
pray they do for time to move.

Surely a life changing place this is,
a chance to do something it gives.

You must keep goodness by your side,
if success is something you desire in life."

TOWN OF DUDLEY SIXTH

Before the recruits was a path in red, a red which coloured the roads and approached the sky. It warned the rookies of the danger they faced in the camp, trying to drive them away. The corpses of former soldiers, which were scattered across the plain, did serve to get the message across. It seemed a battle had recently ensued between the defence forces and the 'outsiders'. However, the walls seemed to be intact, did that suggest the enemy had found a way over? There was nothing to indicate what had actually happened, but the situation had been dealt with after all, so there was not much to worry about. Meanwhile corpses were being cleared by a few soldiers, while others were hard at work building the walls higher. Everyone did the job that was designated to them; there was no time for moaning or mourning. With no possible escape, the rookies were trapped.

For the time being, the rookies were asked to stay in their rooms until everything was back under control. This was applicable to all the rookies, as they had been brought from different regions of the city, all in separate vehicles. They were led to their designated block, by a guide that took the shortest route possible. The darkness of the area could not only be seen but also felt, in the areas the street lamps had been damaged or demolished during the combat, as the stares of many dark beings ruptured deep into the skin of the rookies. They were fresh meat, served in a platter to a hungry prey. Despite being the furthest from the walls, they felt no safer, as they realised the true dangers of being at the camp.

Given the circumstances, it took a few days to reinforce the walls and setup extra precautionary measures. During these days, everyone had been tense, ready for battle at the drop of a hat. With things finally under control, the atmosphere was now calmer.

TOWN OF DUDLEY SIXTH

When the camp was once again 'safe', the camp leader came to brief the rookies. He was a glum person, whose dark skin had aged a lot more than Sambol had expected. The burden of being a leader was getting to him, clearly visible through the sleep deprived look on his face. Being a man of few words, he only gave his name as Asmoth, alongside the instructions to stay in their room until an officer came to guide them for the day's task. He also told them they could not go to any other block without the permission of a high ranking official and someone to supervise them on their trip.

The following day, the leading officer summoned the rookies to a meeting in the hall. Before the meeting they were all given a uniform, which included a shirt, coat, helmet and trouser made of thick materials with camouflage patterns on them, so as to match the colour of the barren land, alongside light brown shoes. Every individual was provided with an army timepiece that they were to wear at all times, unless they had a watch of similar standard. Of course Sambol didn't need one; his watch was much more precise than the recommended amount. Finally, when they were all ready, they were lead to the hall by an officer. The lead officer rose from his chair to give his speech, once everyone in the hall had settled down.

It was a compulsory event, so all late arrivals would be punished. Fortunately, enough, no one was late for their first meeting. The leading officer orated, "I welcome you all to the Defence Department. My name is Rolbus and I am the leading officer at the camp. As you are all aware, our objective is to hold out the enemy, in simpler terms our purpose is to keep them from breaking into the city- from the western front. I want to make it very clear that this is not child's play, we expect you to

TOWN OF DUDLEY SIXTH

work hard to achieve your goal. There are five golden rules here that you must absolutely adhere to, for your own safety and the safety of those around you. Firstly, do not break your ranks unnecessarily, as the mistake of an individual can cost the whole unit. The second rule is to stay alert at all times; **never** try to take on the enemy alone. Here at the camp, we emphasise teamwork, as we try to prioritise survival. Thirdly, talking is prohibited during duty, as we want you to fully focus on the task at hand. The fourth rule is to always be equipped with some sort of weapon/equipment to confront the enemy- never let down your guard. Last of all, report any suspicious activity inside the camp immediately, never investigate by yourself!"

After a few moments of silence Rolbus continued on to say, "Other than that if there is any problem, feel free to discuss it with any officer. Any questions, anyone?"

To which he got the collective reply, "No, Sir!"

With that, officer Rolbus departed with a smile creeping on his face. 'This was going to be fun' he thought. Following his lead, the other officers also left the hall, soon after which the fresher's were asked to go back to their designated rooms.

The following day, the fresher's were lead to the rookie blocks armoury. Here their weapons were to be upgraded to military standards, or be replaced altogether. Sambol and the others handed over their weapons, while receiving replacements. They would be using these as substitutes, until their weapons were returned. Soon after, they were assigned a daily schedule for the training they would receive. That marked the

TOWN OF DUDLEY SIXTH

beginning of their training. The day began with a morning run through the block, all around it and back to the hall. Here, they would each be randomly selected for the training sessions that day.

Being a little late today, they were excused from participating in the morning run (they had already missed it). Instead they were to begin with the training sessions. The one Sambol was told to join was focusing on silent moving techniques, such as crouching and crawling on the ground. Crawling was more painful because it limited his movement and caused leg cramps, and rookies had to spend a lot of time to cover a relatively small distance. As was to be expected, they were punished for moving too slow or not discreetly enough.

It was, according to his brain, an 'utterly useless' exercise. It was not as if they were going to perform a sneak attack on the enemy. But he was in no position to complain, so he was forced to complete the task. Being a little late into the training, he had missed the formations they had taught, so he had to figure things out visually and by his gut. Luckily, he was not being watched when he made mistakes. Once he figured the formation out, he corrected his posture and position. The catch to the exercise was that if anyone moved out of line, preventing others from maintaining their position, they would all be punished. Whenever someone challenged him, the training officer repeated, "Today's lesson is how your actions affect others."

It wasn't long before it was time to eat. Dinner was served in the hall, an average looking place with light shining through the windows, from the lamps outside. It was empty, other than the presence of a few tables and chairs. The only downside to the place- was that the room was filled with straw, evidence that it was previously used as a barn. The barn had become a part of the rookie block, as the structure was built around its sides and front.

The hunger gnawing at the fresher's turned them into zombies, so there was no push or shoves- as the fatigue dampened their aggression. The food was distributed by a simple first come- first serve rule.

Sambol was busy feasting himself on a large meal. He hadn't had such a satisfying meal even during his days back at home. His temporary joy was replaced by memories of his family when he thought about home. He felt home-sick, but he was far from his family- unable to see them. He wished he would see them soon, but that was not possible. But he would see them after his service ended, with that in mind he vowed to work hard to complete his year of service.

Around him at a table sat some other recruits Sambol had met that were around his age, he enjoyed their company- as they had similar traits to him. They were namely: Gerath, Jonard, Kilurb, Raza and Zain. They all feasted from classic ceramic bowls. It seemed the bowls were from the pre-collision era, as they were decorated to reflect a joyful lifestyle. There were cracks and scratches all over the bowls, but that did not change the fact that these ornaments were there only link to the past.

Finally, when everyone had finished their meal, they all herded near the iron door. The fresher's further from the door were yelling at the ones by the door, asking things such as, 'what's the holdup?' or 'just open the door

TOWN OF DUDLEY SIXTH

already'. Until someone, from the crowd by the door, exclaimed, "The door is locked, it won't budge!"

"Try harder!" some said, as the shock of being locked in was not welcoming for the rookies. But Sambol and his companions remained calmly seated at the table, thinking things over in a calm fashion. "Looks like another training exercise," said Kilurb, who was seated with a smile on his face.

His intelligence inspired Sambol, as Kilurb was usually surrounded by hardworking and competitive people. His facial features were prominent; he had violet eyes, under light grey eyebrows, that twinkled with hope. Kilurb was mentally and physically fit. He looked like an old sage, as a result of his platinum-toned round face.

"I kind of expected this, it's just one of those things," replied Gerath, who was a pessimist and always ready for bad situations.

He was the muscle who had a tangerine afro and skin. Gerath was a target for bullying. He was bullied due to a belief of the people from the pre collision era; people who had the same coloured eyes and hair were considered an inferior race. Even in the modern day, the concept was not completely demolished. But Gerath never let the idea bother him too much.

"It seems to me that we have to find another way out. I bet the thick heads are going to use their spoons to dig through the ground and magically make a tunnel to lala land," hypothesized Raza in a sarcastic tone. He was the one who always stated the obvious, albeit in a sarcastic manner.

TOWN OF DUDLEY SIXTH

He was also the one who spoke what was on everyone's mind when they could not. He was a talkative person, was smart and had polished brown eyes, which rested under thin navy eyebrows. Being the youngest amongst the group, he was always assertive.

"Let's have a look around and see what we can do." Sambol urged.

Meanwhile, everyone else was busy looking around the room. 'Good luck to them', Gerath thought, as they found nothing. They wrestled with the door, looked at the floor for a key they could use to open the lock, a key that would be conveniently placed for them to see, only to finally give up and sit back in their seats. The words, "Yes, this is a test. We will be judging everyone on their ability. With this we can then group you with others at the same level, to improve your weak points." caught their attention.

At that point, everyone turned to see Raza talking with a member of staff (retired soldiers), that had stayed behind. The following events were chaotic; everyone rushed to them to ask the staff the way out. "It's not as if the staff is going to tell them, oh look there is the exit, and you can all leave with full marks, for doing absolutely nothing!" exclaimed Gerath. But that taunt made him remember a joke Sambol made, a joke about some of the staff members 'sneaking out', but none of the fresher had given much attention to his words, as they were all too hungry to even think properly.

The 'dummies' were busy bombarding the members of staff with questions, but only got a meek silence in return. It did not take long for them to get bored doing so. On the other hand, Sambol and Kilurb

TOWN OF DUDLEY SIXTH

were feeling the walls, which made Gerath wonder what they were doing. So he got up, approaching Sambol to ask what he was doing. "Oh, I'm surprised you haven't figured it out. It's quite straight forward really, if this was a former barn there must be an open side where there were big wooden doors, so there must be something covering that door, like wallpaper. If we find it, we can tear through it and open the former front door. "

It clicked; it made more sense when he thought of things that way. He then looked around to see where the others were, he saw Jonard dragging some chairs and tables to the back of the room. So he decided to help him. Meanwhile Raza and Zain were looking for something in the straw at the front of the barn.

'Oh well, they could do whatever they wanted to' contemplated Gerath, as he helped Jonard with the chairs. At least it would help him get marks for trying. It did not take them long, to accumulate about half a dozen chairs to the front. When they were done they sat down at the front, waiting for the others to find the door. It only took a few minutes wait, as Kilurb found it. After that, Jonard and Gerath helped Kilurb peel off the paper- with the help of Sambol, in a civilised manner. They had figured that the paper was an important resource, so wasting it would mean less marks.

When the other recruits saw them, they began to get up. All the while they had been looking at Sambol and his companions, as if they were stupid. Now they were rushing towards them. But they were having trouble getting over the tables that blocked their path. It seemed Jonard's and Gerath's hard work was paying off. In that time, Zain and Raza had already made it to the front holding a long rope. They had figured that there should be a rope in the barn. By the time the rookies had overcome the obstacle- the group of six had separated the paper from the door and tied the chairs together. They were bashing the door with the collective chairs, to generally weaken its structure. After a few swings, they stopped to untie the ropes.

Seeing how the others had already made it over the obstacles, they ran into the weakened door a few times. About two minutes later, the rookies had opened a path through it. With the back door broken, the rookies ran out, while Sambol and his friends refrained from being trampled upon. When they finally came out they saw Rolbus standing there beaming. Wickedly, he retorted, "I see there is still some common sense among the young ones. I must have been mistaken about you being be a useless bunch of knuckleheads."

After a small pause he directed a question to the staff, "That was definitely fun, don't you think so too? Well I assume you have graded them properly. The results need to be handed out tomorrow."

Then looking back at the rookies he stated," You may be wandering, why I came all the way here. Well I am here to inform you of a very important event. Starting in two months' time, an event is being held, in which you have to sneakily leave the camp. From there you should head to the town hall, collect a commendation from the head commander and return back. It will be about speed and agility, as we will not go easy on you, the whole way you will be chased. Of course the ones who succeed will get a chance to either visit home or choose a quick promotion with a few bonuses."

TOWN OF DUDLEY SIXTH

Rolbus left shortly after his announcement. With that the fresher's returned back to their abode.

TOWN OF DUDLEY SIXTH

Chapter 7

Broken Ties

Two months passed since the rookies had begun training in the camp. They had learned various things during training. One of the most important things was, being to be ready for any situation. For this reason, they even learned how to wield weapons other than their own. They had been trained thoroughly; no gap had been left in their training. After all they had now been summoned to their last meeting as rookies.

One again, the fresher's were united in the hall, just like when they first arrived. Some of the staff was recognisable- other soldiers were too, including the officers that had taught them. Among the officers, there were Rolbus and Jiva. They stood behind Asmoth, who was waiting for everyone to be seated.

After a long silence, Asmoth spoke in a dull voice, "I am proud to announce that your training as rookies is complete. This year was more fruitful than many others. This credit does not only go to those who trained you but also to you. As all of you are certainly quick learners. Rolbus will brief you on what to expect next."

With that, Asmoth left to resume his other duties, while a beaming devil made his way to the front. Without any further delay, he bellowed, "After being trained so hard, I believe you have earned a little break. You will

TOWN OF DUDLEY SIXTH

have two weeks of rest, but first you will have to collect your armour and modified weapons. Of course, you are advised to use some of your time getting used to your equipment. As once your break is over you will be stationed- as amateurs, among the ranks to defend the city. Considering how you have finished your training a few weeks early, you will have access to the amateur building, as until your break is over, you will stay at the rookie block."

It was a late start for Sambol the following morning; he had collected his armour and weapons yesterday. His gun had been repainted with a firmer paint. The grip had been replaced; a few extra mods had been added including a scope. But it had a name plate that read 'Davince's Abyss', which was not there before. It was still just a gun, but somehow more reliable. His sword had been remodelled into a longer, thinner sword with sharp edges and a point. It also had an added curve. The hilt had been coated with special metals, so as to be denser. It gave the weapon a better balance, making it more manoeuvrable.

That day he wore a fancy shirt under a dull black coat, a pair of denim jeans with a pair of shiny red shoes, a sheathed sword with his gun belt, all to go with his armour. As the armour had been painted with a camouflage pattern, he did not need his camouflaged uniform. Once he was ready, he had a look around the rookie department. Unfortunately, no matter how much

TOWN OF DUDLEY SIXTH

he thought on the event, there was no chance of running without being seen.

There was sandy soil at the back of the block leading to the camp's boundary. The camp's boundary was a huge fence, all around the camp. It had various traps associated with it, but for the event the lethal ones were to be deactivated. But despite that Sambol could not think of a way to avoid being seen. Especially with the watch towers, shining lights towards the blocks 24/7. These were located at different parts of the fence, so that any incoming people would be seen by them.

Tired of racking his brain, he went to the outdoor ground meant for the rookie department's training. On one of the benches he saw Zain, Gerath, and Kilurb talking amongst each other. During the harsh exercises and training regime, they had all become good friends. They talked some, debating on methods to complete the assignment, but not even Kilurb could think of something that they could definitely pull off by themselves.

After dinner, Sambol occupied himself with his watch making tools: a white-gold platinum case, an elinvar hairspring and tourbillon with Inca bloc shock absorbing technology for the mechanical movement were just some of the tool he had at his disposal. It was just about placing them in a proper order. He spent a lot of time making his watch, making sure he didn't miss any details.

TOWN OF DUDLEY SIXTH

Doing so reminded him of Eric (the watchmaker next-door). He certainly hoped to see him again sometime soon, maybe he would choose to go home as his reward, if he somehow performed that miraculous feat. It would give him a chance to meet his parents, Lazlo and Arantus. If he had some time to spare, he would definitely spend some with Eric.

When he quit for the day, he went to the extra room in the block where there were board games and other fun activities and spent the remainder of the day there. It was more enjoyable when he spotted Raza there. They enjoyed games of chess and draughts to pass the time. After all they had not really enjoyed these games in their childhood, because some of the wood in the pieces and other such materials were considered 'valuable resources'. Meaning that, these were all taken from households. Only one of each board game was kept, due to the insistence of some that it was a valuable part of their heritage.

Soon after, he went to meet his friends, who banded together in Jonard's room. They all left their shoes in a corner, as they didn't want to add to Jonard's chores. They then discussed random topics, such as watches, vehicles, and the condition of the city- when someone mentioned the upcoming challenge, as well as how the weather was as bad as always. But when they came around to the topic of the event, no one could think of a way to escape. To lighten up the mood Raza suggested moving to Sambol's room and to also get a look at his work.

TOWN OF DUDLEY SIXTH

While in Sambol's room, everyone talked, except Gerath. He was looking through the drawers for his watch. He was in a hurry to find the watch and Sambol was not disclosing its location. Until he noticed the watch parts inside a tray, hidden by loose sheets on top. Taking the tray, he showed everyone the parts. Seeing the tray in Gerath's hand, alerted Sambol. "Put that back where you found it! It is not for show yet! C'mon guys, this is not cool!"

After Gerath's continuous waving it around, a sigh escaped Sambol as he warned, "Okay, you can look, but be careful with it."

They all admired his work and were secretly jealous for his craftiness. He had a talent and a very steady hand, skills that distinguished his work from other timepieces, both modern and from the pre-collision era. And so the rest of the day was spent rather gleefully.

TOWN OF DUDLEY SIXTH

Chapter 8
A Day off Duty

Today was the last day of the break. The rookies were transferred to the amateur block and shown their new rooms. Due to the change in blocks, the rookie block would be once again used as a store. It was an ideal location to keep equipment. Seeing how the 'new amateurs' were late for dinner because of the building change, they were served dinner in their rooms.

After having a pleasant meal, Zain heard a knock on his door. He expected someone to come in and tell him about training, but before him stood a beaming Jonard. He had come to invite Zain to the arcade in the building. Jonard had told Zain that, he would wait for him by the stairs leading to the arcade, whilst he collected the weekly allowance. He then waited for Zain for quite a while; he certainly didn't hesitate to mention his impatience to him when Zain arrived.

A bronze door with patterns in a dark brown chocolate PVD awaited them at the top of the stairs. The door was twice as high as Zain, which made it difficult for him to twist the knob, so Jonard had to open it. Once they were inside they noticed the use of glowing liquid to illuminate the room.

After purchasing tickets, which were worth a few hours of playtime, they began to lose themselves in the majestic glamour of the place. They started off with Ludo, which Jonard was much better at playing, but they both enjoyed the game. Moving onto chess was better for Zain because he was a good tactician. Jonard moved his pieces

TOWN OF DUDLEY SIXTH

a little carelessly, falling into Zain's trap. Zain usually broke his formation to win the game. However, the boys were not competitive, which made their time at the arcade exhilarating.

Mechanical pinball was next; the points were represented by different coloured bearings that fell into a visible chamber. These were then returned into the mechanism by placing the right bearings into the correct bearing reservoir. They both enjoyed the game; it was well worth the trouble. Although Zain could keep the ball occupied longer, he did not usually score as many points as Jonard.

Time whizzed by as they both lost their selves in fun and games. Feeling hungry, Zain went to the café and bought an aged oak with herbs and hot water. Unfortunately, there was no café in the rookie block- although rationing still applied to them now it was better to choose it. So he also bought some food for Jonard, who was busy at a different game. This is why Zain left his food at the table with his coat.

Next, Zain went to the workout place, where he spent some time working on his form. He met Gerath who asked for Jonard, so he told him that Jonard was at the arcade. While working out he spotted Raza, so he went over. They both trained hard to get in form. Zain told Raza that he was finding it rather difficult to move 'flexibly' in his armour. He also asked Raza how he found his equipment and armour.

To which Raza replied, "I do agree that the armour does restrict movement a little, but it is still worthwhile to utilise. On the other hand, my weapons were definitely modified in a proper manner. They are definitely more

TOWN OF DUDLEY SIXTH

efficient in combat. I know that you chose completely new weapons from their stock, how do you find your weapons."

"I prefer these over my previous ones, I had a little difficulty getting used to them. But I am sure it will pay off." stated Zain.

They went on to talk about ideal situations for them to use different weapons and how the defence department had a large stock of weapons. It seemed things could not be more ordinary for a nation affected by a collision, while also being the last ones to survive.

Sometimes, Zain thought whether survival was even worthwhile, was it even worth struggling. Of course it was, at least that was what he told himself. Anything that could make him sleep easy at night would help; even a lie to himself was worthwhile if it fulfilled that purpose. So after he had exercised to his heart's content, Zain went to his room and got ready for bed. He wanted to get an early start on the next day, so he would rest for now. Seeing how his brain was questioning things, it would be a while before he would drift into sleep.

Chapter 8
Back Home (Part 2)

Back at Sambol's home, Grumlov's heart was heavy with grief. He wished with his heart, that his daughter Engelia and son Sambol were here. He knew that Engelia would cope well with her role. She was the one he favoured over his other children, for her responsible attitude. Sambol was exactly the opposite, like a rebel working to do the opposite of whatever he was told. Unfortunately, reverse psychology did not work on him, Grumlov thought with a smile.

But he wasn't all bad, he had carried forward his interests in mechanical technology, and he respected him. That was enough to show his love towards his father. Grumlov had become self-absorbed over the years. The sight of people dying before him had had its toll. He was mentally disturbed by what he had seen during his year of service. He had tried to stop Sambol from sharing the same destiny, but he had always known Sambol to be even stronger than he had imagined. As a result of the year of service, Grumlov experienced nightmares and mood swings.

He prayed that his children would not be affected in the manner he was, as that was all he could do in his condition. The first few days after their departure he had refused to take his medicine, which was detrimental to his health. Moranta would stand next to him all day with the medicine and water in hand until her own health began to deteriorate. That was enough to get through the lapse Grumlov was stuck in. Ever since that day, he knows took his medicine on a daily basis.

TOWN OF DUDLEY SIXTH

Lazlo and Arantus had helped comfort Moranta, she was equally sad about the departure of her children, but had stayed strong. It showed her determination and strong will. Her sons had convinced her things would get better. She was worried about Engelia and hoped she returned safely. But she had faith in her, the belief that she could make it through.

Sambol was also constantly on her mind. She worried about him more, because he was naïve and did not understand the world as he should. He wasn't aware of the injustice in this world; not everyone would fight him on equal grounding or fight fairly. His profession was too dangerous for his own good. So she prayed for his safe return, for it was all she could do.

With the departure of Sambol and Engelia, the house was not as lively as it used to be. Opposed to the happiness it boasted in their presence, it now had a glum atmosphere around it.

TOWN OF DUDLEY SIXTH

Chapter 9
Amidst Confusion

Many people were skilled in traditional weapons such as spears, javelins, or bows and arrows. However, Sambol was more of a gun person, which is why he was stationed on top of the rear tower of defence. The towers served as an extra line of defence; there purpose was to counter a breach through the wall.

The city walls were the ideal location for the primary watch towers. In order to keep watch on the movement of any hostile forces and to predict attacks. Behind the primary watch towers was another row of towers lined with cannons and other heavy weapons to counter a frontal attack. The rear towers were a line of defence where everyone could fall back, reassemble with backup, and retaliate.

As of now the amateurs were given the task to patrol the rear towers. Anxiety built up inside Sambol, causing him to jump every time he heard an abnormal sound. Sweat began to slide down his forehead. He was too tense, fortunately the day passed by quite calmly. The following days Sambol began to relax while on duty. Not as much as to hinder his role though, as he knew the consequences of slipping up. The punishment for slackers and for people, who made mistakes during duty, was the job of polishing weapons and armour and other menial chores.

After doing his rounds, Sambol returned to the Amateur block, looking for his friends. He wanted to ask them, if they had thought about the coming up event. He had a look at Zain's, Raza's and Jonard's room, but they were empty. Causing him to wonder what they were up

TOWN OF DUDLEY SIXTH

Amidst Confusion

to, it took him a while to find them all. They were all gathered in Kilurb's room. It seemed they had come up with a plan.

An hour later, they were ready to execute the plan they had come up with, at any moment. But the most ideal moment would be during the change in shift. So until then they would have to continue with their duties. As it was quite the peaceful day; Sambol avoided the troublesome amateurs more than he usually did. While trying to keep his excitement under control, he did his rounds until his break finally arrived. But today time had stretched a little long; it had almost come to a complete stop.

He was currently headed to the cafe, as that was the meeting place for his group of comrades. It would also be time for the shift change at the border in ten minutes. As he had expected, the group was seated at a table, waiting for his arrival. Seeing how Sambol just did not have much luck with time, it seemed like he was late yet again.

"So now that you're finally here, let's get going." was the first thing Gerath said.

As they got up to leave, the towers' bells began to toll. It seemed something was wrong, perhaps another group of mutants made it inside the city walls. So as to answer the many questions in their heart, Sambol and the others went outside to get a look at the situation.

The site before them was a horrific one. Through the large magnifying glass that was placed at the rear tower, they saw many of the defence department had fallen as the wall and the primary towers had been

TOWN OF DUDLEY SIXTH

Amidst Confusion

completely demolished. It was too late to fight back. Which was why they could be seen slowly retreating, whilst the secondary tower kept the enemy distracted. They could only hold out for so long, they needed to sit tight, at least until reinforcements arrived.

Hurriedly the amateurs marched towards the rear tower, where Rolbus was to brief them. Upon arrival, they met Rolbus and Jiva. But something felt wrong; they did not look their normal selves.

It was not until Rolbus spoke in small bursts, not making much sense, that the severity of the situation became clear. "You have all trained hard to get to this point. I am sure Asmoth would have been proud of you all. Especially the new batch, considering how quickly you have all completed your initial training. Asmoth was fighting on the frontline, trying to buy us all time to rally our forces for a counter attack. They had already taken out the wall and the lookouts. We could not hold out, so we all had to retreat. We will not fare well without backup." Rolbus said in an honest soft tone.

From the way he spoke, it was obvious what had happened. To make things easier for him, all they could do was listen in silence. Rolbus then continued on to say, "Looking at our situation, we would need some soldiers to go to the head council. So as to ask for some backup, even if it is patrol officers or retired personnel with military experience. It seems that it is time to go all out. This role is best suited to the new recruits. While the others can equip this tower, gather the supplies and survey the enemy. The secondary tower is half a kilometre from here, so in the time it takes for the enemy to arrive, we should be fully prepared. This time we are

TOWN OF DUDLEY SIXTH

not looking at a few mutants, we are facing an army of mutants and rogue survivors. "

With that, they were dismissed. Following which a grief-stricken Rolbus left for the battle, to fulfil his duty; which currently required him to lead a whole camp in battle. He went towards the thick smoke, the battle cries and the sound of death. The cries and screams of agony had filled the air, as had the evil cackles and groans of the oncoming slaughter house. The grim reaper himself would have begun to fear death if he saw the battle in person. Some individuals had surpassed death by the grim reaper; they had become what they once feared. It was certainly a day of great importance, as the outcome today would decide the future tomorrow.

Back at the rear tower Jiva was busy guiding the amateurs, issuing commands and distributing duties. Meanwhile, Sambol, Zain and Raza were asked to take a letter to the head commander. It had information on the current crisis and called for reinforcements from the stand by units- stationed close to the centre of Lukemilldale. On the other hand, Kilurb, Gerath and Jonard were asked to head towards the mayors so as to call in people with military experience and patrolling officers into battle.

The group of friends rushed down the stairs, heading towards the rookie block. As things were, the major traps had been disabled at the borderline between the camp and the city. Also if there were traitors in the midst or enemy spies in the area, they would have to sneak out. But the alarm would go off once they stepped outside the border. This meant they would have to execute their plan perfectly. Keeping in mind only two at a time could cross the plain. Jiva had told them that if

TOWN OF DUDLEY SIXTH

Amidst Confusion

more than two crossed they would fall into a vast pit set close to the border. It was a weight trap set for the enemy, to stall them if need be. But it could also trap the defence forces on this side, as they could not risk showing the enemy the way to avoid the trap. At the cost of sacrificing themselves they could prevent the whole city from falling.

Zain and Gerath were the first ones to head towards the border. They were crouched and moved briskly towards their goal. Their movement was neither too slow nor too fast, as they had to avoid any traps for discreetness as well as to save time. Once they were there, they headed towards the evacuation exit that was closest to them. Typing in the correct code opened the door. Zain made sure it stayed open, while Gerath used Sambol's tools on the dial (for entering the code) to remove the front face- which he did with the help of his muscles, to separate a few gears from the system. Disabling the mechanism for the door, he then did the same to the mechanism for the alarm which was by the door, covered in dirt. It took him a while to find it, but he eventually did.

Once that was done the two waited outside for the others. Next Kilurb and Raza left towards the exit. Finally, Sambol and Jonard were moving towards the others. Sambol was very careful stepping on places he had seen the others step upon. He was confident and began to move faster, when suddenly he got a tap on the shoulder. Drawing his gun, he swivelled only to see Jonard was stuck in a trap. His leg was stuck in a rubber clamp that was tightening its grip by the second. Sambol had to do something soon. He drew his sword and began cutting the rubber, but that was too slow. With no choice left he drew his gun, attached to it a silencer and after aiming

TOWN OF DUDLEY SIXTH

appropriately he shot the rubber to weaken it. After which he pulled the rubber apart with his hands long enough for Jonard to remove his leg.

Seeing how his blood had not been circulating his leg properly and how the bullet had grazed him. Jonard could not move immediately. It would take him some time to recover, but time was not ticking in their favour. So Sambol had to make a quick decision, leave him there or somehow get him across. But he could not think of a way to get him across, until an idea hit him.

He asked Jonard, "Could you do me a favour and lie down?"

To which Jonard replied, "Anything you say, boss."

"Now slowly move your healthy leg up, making sure you don't pull a muscle. Don't want to immobilise you."

Once Jonard had raised his leg to a reasonable height he said, "That's as much as I can do, you better not be pulling my leg"

"I am not pulling your leg, I am serious about what I am thinking and it isn't dragging you slowly across the land."

Having said that, Sambol was not sure it would actually work. But he had to try. So he lay down his supplies bag, which had tyres on it, tied Jonard's chest to the top of the bag. Then took his good leg and began to swiftly move towards the exit, all the while he remained crouched. Within a few minutes they had made it. By the time they reached the exit, Jonard had gained enough rest

TOWN OF DUDLEY SIXTH

to move a little by himself. As such Kilurb and Gerath supported him and took off towards their goal.

On the other hand, Sambol, Zain and Raza had chosen to head towards a car station, collect a car and drive to the town hall. As Sambol was more knowledgeable about mechanical technology he could figure out a way to use a car. When they finally arrived, they noticed that most of the cars were in bad shape, but still all of them were locked. Sambol looked among the cars and chose one that he thought would still be mobile. But there was the problem that it was locked.

Fortunately, Zain had a little trick up his sleeve, using a paperclip, needle, and toothpick he always had on him, he picked the door lock. Once the door was open, they had to start it to see if it even worked. Sambol wound the mechanism via the gearbox and pressed the pedal to get the gears running- as he had seen his father do. Eventually after a few tries they got the engine rumbling. Sambol sat in the front, whereas he advised Raza and Zain to sit in the back- buckle their seatbelts and grab on to something. They thought he was just exaggerating, but still buckled their seatbelts to not dissuade him.

What they did not expect was Sambol to accelerate the car full throttle. It took some time for them to notice, but they could also hear an engine at the back. That got them panicking, the car began to skid on turns. The vehicle was obviously not stable; it knocked down a lamppost here, a post box there. When they got onto the straight road from the west to the town hall, Sambol sped up to the car's maximum speed; two hundred and twenty yards per second.

TOWN OF DUDLEY SIXTH

When the car arrived at the town hall in a few minutes, Sambol's passengers were more than happy to leave the vehicle. They fell onto the ground, straight after opening the door. It took them a minute or two to collect themselves.

Once they had finally recovered they made their way to the door. However, the two guards posted at the entrance acted as an obstacle. Of course, they would not believe the words of the amateurs- about the attack. They would probably have the document checked for authenticity. Then after confirming it was real, they would get entry. Even that depended on the honesty of the personnel who handled the letter. In short it was too risky and would take too much time. So they did the one thing they could in the situation. They caught them by surprise.

Zain used his throwing skills to hurtle a pair of linked chains at the feet of the guard that was closer to them and then he ran straight by, after pushing him so as to make him fall over. It got the guard to chase him, but perhaps he had overdone the 'distraction' as the guard didn't look as if he was going to let this slide. However, the other guard remained perfectly calm, maintaining his position. Meanwhile Sambol ran to open the door and Raza tackled the other guard- an offense that could cost him his life, but could save many others.

Once the door was open, Sambol gave the other two the signal after which they all rushed towards him, friends and angry guards included. Together the friends ascended the stairs in frenzy with the guards sharp on their tail. They burst into the first room they could enter, in which a meeting of the head council was taking place. The first person to notice them was the head commander.

TOWN OF DUDLEY SIXTH

Amidst Confusion

Without wasting a moment, Raza exclaimed a string of words that came out as a single sound, before the head commander could utter a single word. Raza exclaimed, "We can explain, we are here to convey an extremely important message. The western border is under a full on frontal attack, one which our forces alone cannot hold out against. We came to call on for reinforcements. The details are in this letter."

With that, Raza took the letter from Sambol and handed it to a royal guard, who then gave it to the head commander. The whole room was in utter silence, the heavy breaths of the three arrivals were the one thing hanging in the air. Not even the guards moved to drag the amateurs out of the town hall. Everyone's eyes were on the head commander, as he read through the letter.

The contents seemed to have a deep effect on him, as he grew pale upon reading it. It took him a while to muster the instructions "Leave us, you are dismissed," directed towards the guards.

After a brief silence, he continued, "Follow me lads."

Following which they were lead towards the next room, all the while the head commander was having a conversation with his advisor. It seemed they spoke in code words, as what they said could not be understood by the three friends.

As they proceeded towards an unspecified destination, for no apparent reason- the amateurs were more than perplexed. It took Raza a little courage to say, "No offence, Sir, but this better be important. Every minute wasted means more casualties," to which he got

TOWN OF DUDLEY SIXTH

no response and an elbow to his stomach from Sambol. But he had done nothing wrong, so he made a face so as to say 'What?' to Sambol. To which Sambol stared at him, as if trying to say, you are supposed to trust and respect the head commander.

Chapter 10
Sword of Hope

The group of survivors were headed towards the centre of the town hall; they went from room to room, every step bringing them closer to their destination. When suddenly, a dead end appeared before the survivors; as was to be expected they were brought to a halt. The head commander and his advisor began to talk among themselves again, this time it sounded like they were having a debate.

Throughout the discussion, the amateurs had been alienated. They were not aware of what the discussion was about, who was stalling the conversation or even who was more dominant. It took quite some time, before the two talking amongst each other came to a conclusion.

Once their conversation was over, the head commander turned around to say, "I know that the breach is a matter of utmost urgency, but do understand that I must brief you on the importance of what lies on the other side of this wall. As you already know, I am Nartejj, head commander of the legendary warriors. What you need to know is the history of the role. Back in the early days after the collision, there was a lot of panic- as the chance of a collision was never even considered a possibility. The people were proud of the celestial defences and had overestimated them."

After a brief gap, Nartejj continued his briefing, "The situation changed people and they became more barbaric. We lost many good souls in those days. The only thing that could change that was a leader. There were a lot of people willing to lead; those who did succeed lived short lives with little progress made in establishing peace and order. It was not until James Woodward became Head Commander that things changed. He was the one who came up with the departments and implemented the ranking system we know live by. Thanks to his efforts, we and the residents are alive. However, due to the excessive criticism his actions received, James resigned, declaring me as the next successor. That was seven years ago. Even today he is alive, standing before you as my elder and advisor."

With that, Nartejj stopped knocking on different parts of the wall. He hurriedly turned and advised everyone to move back. Just as he had done so, there was the sound of a click. Then there was a painful silence. Followed by a deep pitch of sound, that came from the rotation of heavy gears. The scene before them was majestic, the entire wall before them rotated to reveal a hidden door. After punching in the password, James opened the door.

Once they were through the door: Sambol, Zain and Raza found themselves in a narrow corridor leading deeper towards the centre of the building. At the other end of the corridor, there was an old door covered in rust, due to lack of use. With great care, Nartejj opened this door, leading them to what seemed to be an empty room.

Until Sambol saw it; hanging from the ceiling was an upside down sword. It appeared to be lodged deep within the ceiling, only part of the hilt was visible from below. Zain was perplexed to see it, whereas Raza acted as if it were perfectly normal, for the head commander to lead them to a room with a sword stuck in the roof, at such an important time. Sambol had not even decided what to feel, he was at a point where he was questioning Nartejj's sanity.

Ignorant of the awe it received, the head commander stepped towards it. Until he was only a few centimetres from it, he then remarked, "Our first leader found this in Tenebris Mundo. It was the one thing that made him leader. Unfortunately, he was using this room to practice with it and it got stuck in the roof. Humiliated, he kept the truth from the people, saying it was kept at the centre of the town hall for its safety. Due to the instability his lie caused, he ran into Tenebris Mundo. A few years later, a scavenger found his corpse. Since then, we have kept this matter a secret. All of the previous Head Commanders have tried to free it, as it is said to be able to cut through even the toughest of substances, but none have succeeded. It is the only thing we can use to boost the morale of our men and easily cut through the mutants."

Nartejj then grabbed the handle, took a few breaths and pulled it with all his might. But to no avail, as it did not budge, sighing he said, "Looks like we are going to have to break the wall around it, it isn't going to come out so easily, this is probably a waste of time, but there is no harm in trying. "

The head commander walked towards James to look through the tools he had brought with him, for something they could use to break the wall. Just as he had turned his back, Zain ran to the sword in an attempt to free it. Once Sambol saw him run, he tried to intercept Zain, but Zain was seen.

TOWN OF DUDLEY SIXTH

Bubbling with rage, James grabbed him by his collar, lifting him inches off the ground. All the while yelling at him, for trying to insult the head commander and himself, but Sambol was not aware of a word being said. He instinctively tried to defend his friend; he did so by gripping the sword hilt and yanking it free with the force of each and every muscle in his body. Only to hold it to the throat of the head councillor's advisor, warning him, "You let him go now, or I certainly won't leave you unscathed."

Nartejj heard the ruckus and proceeded to pull James to the side saying, "He's only a child, it was the most obvious and normal thing to do. He felt he was special, so he tried, as did I... " but his speech slurred upon seeing the sword in Sambol's hand. The scene hit him as a dream at first, but as time progressed his jaw dropped- upon realizing it was no dream. Then he just smiled, with a mysterious twinkle in his eyes.

Meanwhile, James went pale seeing the sword in his hands. When Sambol finally realised what he was holding, he almost dropped the sword, juggling with it until he was finally back in control. With his voice quivering he stated, "I'm serious, step away from Zain!"

Upon which Nartejj burst into laughter. Laughing he pulled at James's shoulder; as if to ask him to step back. James began to stare at him; it was not helping him that the head councilor- the one whose respect he was trying to emphasise, was laughing his head off, as if he were crazy. It took him long enough to calm down. When he finally came back to his senses, Nartejj responded to James glare with the words, "Perhaps it was not a waste of time after all; fate is at work here young one. However, the battle rages on, we must hurry." A worried expression

TOWN OF DUDLEY SIXTH

showed itself towards the end of his speech. "As for you James, that behavior was out of line. You should apologise to the boy and take care in the future. Let us ready the reinforcements."

The group of five hurriedly returned to the meeting room. Nartejj asked one of the guards to summon the reinforcements stationed at the defence department, a building next to the town hall. Meanwhile, Sambol along with the other two amateurs were asked to depart with the car 'they borrowed', so as to inform the soldiers that reinforcements were to arrive. They would also help in stalling the enemy. Accompanying them would be all the guards stationed at the town hall who were ready for combat. Of course, not all of them had cars- the 'resources' used had to be considered after all.

Once again, Sambol swiveled the car left and right until they arrived at the massacre. The city's fighters had backed up to the last line of towers, where they kept the enemy at bay. Sambol was focused on his destination, as he rushed towards the battlefield. Trying to keep up with him were Raza and Zain, but for some reason he appeared to run faster than they remembered. However, he had kept his sword in a sheath, as advised by Nartejj.

Some soldiers moved out of the way as Sambol ran towards them. When he arrived at the top of the tower, he saw Jonard helping others load the cannons. Gerath was aiming at the enemy with his sniper rifle and firing his gun, whereas Kilurb was busy firing orders. Sambol was then informed that after Asmoth had been lost to them, Rolbus had stepped up in his place. In his place, Jiva had been promoted to lead officer. But Rolbus had been injured; consequently, he had been escorted to the rookie department to heal, once some reinforcements arrived. It seemed Jonard, Kilurb and Gerath had come back with the reinforcements.

In his stead, Kilurb and Jiva were collectively giving out orders and handling his duties. But they were not the only ones being led by tacticians. The enemy had begun to spread out. The heavily built ones were at the base of the towers attacking the base of the tower. Meanwhile, another unit was collecting the ammunition and other equipment left by the defence department in the secondary tower- things left behind during their retreat.

Sambol was asked by Kilurb to use his gun and handed a sniper rifle, to help take care of the forces attacking the base. He ordered Gerath and Zain, to use the cannons when necessary to fire at the enemy, without doing any excessive damage to the tower itself. If the backup arrived, they would be able to take on the threat more effectively.

It seemed that the enemy number was not being affected, as more rogue survivors and mutants replaced the ones that had been dealt with. At the moment, the defense department was not suffering heavy losses. Other than the occasional boulders and what not hurled their way by catapults- the occasional bullet, spear, arrow and any other weapon capable of dealing damage cost them casualties. Aside from the few that used the weapons the defense department left behind to fight, the others were not much of a threat as individuals from that distance.

It was not long before further reinforcements arrived. Nartejj was leading, followed shortly by James and many others. As he arrived, the other soldiers also fell behind him. As soon as he reached the tower, Kilurb

TOWN OF DUDLEY SIXTH

and Jiva updated him on the latest. All the while his expression was unreadable. At the end of the exchange, Nartejj ordered the soldiers to fall back and open the doors. They would rush the enemy with all they had. At least at a shorter range, they would be safe from the catapults.

Sambol assessed the situation, weighed his options on how and who to fight first, when the gates of the tower opened. Of course, the enemy was left confused by the open invitation. Sambol fired bullet after bullet at the oncoming herd of foes.

The manner in which the situation had reversed in favor of the defense department, it boosted the morale of the soldiers. The prospect for victory was becoming more doable. They managed to push back the enemy to the second tower where a heated battle was now taking place. The defense department fought courageously, as they began to gain the upper hand in combat.

After a few hours of combat, it became clear that the defense department was going to win the battle. By then, even the rogue survivors knew that this battle was lost to them. They had already begun their retreat, with the defenders of Lukemilldale right behind them. Soon they were approaching the city walls, but the scenario before them horrified them. Standing beside the demolished walls were four mutants and a dozen rogue survivors.

But something was wrong with the mutants; they looked different to what the normal invaders looked like. An ear piercing roar suddenly resonated in the air as one of the mutants began to grow bigger; its muscles were expanding and becoming more tense- almost as if his skin

TOWN OF DUDLEY SIXTH

was becoming tougher. Its eyes were rolling above into his head as it looked up at the sky, showing that the mutant had no control over what he was doing. Perhaps it cursed its own fate, or was too agonized by the pain to know what it was doing. What was wrong with the mutant? That was the one thought that terrified the fighters of Lukemilldale, possibly a question they did not want answered.

Then, the same thing happened to the other three mutants; some started later than the others and took longer- to evolve. That was right; the mutants were evolving, something the residents of Lukemilldale had not expected in their wildest dreams. It already took a large group of men to par with one. It might take an army to fight an evolved mutant; and there were four, alongside the rogue survivors.

One was fat and moved slowly towards them. It was the first to head in their direction, but soon ended at the rear of the enemy's formation. Wielding a gigantic staff that was on fire, the mutant was nothing less than a one-man army. Another transformed being was tall, had a giant double sided axe and shield, it played with his weapons as if thinking of grotesque ways to kill them as painfully as possible.

The most troublesome mutant was a frail-looking being that moved quickly. It had started to clear its way through friend and foe with two blades. Following shortly behind was a short, tough being, who used a war hammer to brutally crush those who dared to cross its path.

Jonard was the first to run towards the freaks of nature that were deformed beyond recognition. But he ran towards them from their side. Their eyeballs stared coldly, deep into the onlooker's skin. An ever creepy smile glued to their face. They were hellish monsters, here to do the grim reapers bidding. The first one to clash blades with Jonard was the tall entity, but its axe was having a tough time tackling the two scythe blades used by Jonard.

Sambol thought it was time; time to use the sword. A gun would not be very effective, judging by the situation- brute traditional weapons were the best option. The evolved mutants had skins tougher than steel. Gerath was stalling the short one using a halberd and whip, while Zain used a crossbow to provide cover for him. Kilurb and Raza fought the frail foe with the help of the reinforcements. Kilurb manipulated a ring sword with the aid of his triple sai sword technique, fighting with it as if it were a boomerang. While Raza used a club that was used more like a war hammer.

Giving a fierce war cry, Sambol unsheathed his sword, drawing it to his side. Following which he bulldozed towards the tall one, racing towards the evolved mutant with the desire to defeat it. Noticing the backup, he was going to receive Jonard used his scythe to trap the mutants axe. It gave Sambol the perfect opening, one he planned on using well. With one foul strike he hacked at the enemy in an attempt to cut it in half, but his sword was met with the resistant of its tough skin and it slid across the surface.

But it was not a waste, as it gave the enemy a deep wound. In retaliation the being whacked at Sambol with his shield, which threw him into the air, off his feet. At the same time, it freed its axe from Jonard's tackle, grazing Jonard's shoulder in the process. Jonard was distracted for that moment and almost failed to notice the sword that was sent flying past him, which then embedded itself

TOWN OF DUDLEY SIXTH

into the new found being's chest. An ear piercing shriek escaped its mouth, which was now telling the tale of the pain it felt.

In the time it took the being to recollect itself, Sambol was back. With the sniper in his possession, Sambol shot the tall enemy at point black range at its kneecap. Even if it did not pierce the skin, it was definitely good enough to cause some internal damage. Through the corner of his eye, Sambol only just managed to see a blur as the being threw its shield behind Sambol, blocking his path and smashed him with the axe. His gun did not offer much strength as he used it to block the attack. It broke into two, but the pressure of the blow had burrowed him slightly into the ground. He would not be able to evade the next one, as his feet were stuck in the ground.

It seemed that this was it for Sambol; perhaps his father had been right. He was no hero- he was not even good enough to be average. All he could think was what his father would have done in that situation. While he was thinking that, he noticed the sword lodged into the skin of the target before him. In a desperate attempt to free it, he moved forward gripping the hilt. As he did so, he saw the incoming axe that would soon end his life. With no other choice he yanked at the sword, but it was not budging.

The axe was only a few inches away; Sambol had already accepted the prospect of death and had closed his eyes. But he was not divaricated; all he heard was the sound of metal contacting metal. Opening his eyes, he saw the being had been disarmed by Jonard's' dead scythes. With the fresh prospect of survival in mind,

Sambol gave the sword a firm yank and slashed in an upwards motion, cutting the enemy in two.

At last one enemy was down. But there were still many left behind. When he looked among the soldiers he saw many of the defense department had fallen, but not in vain. One of the evolved mutants had been defeated by James Woodward and Nartejj; they had caused enough internal damage for the insides of the chubby beast to come gushing out. In his range of vision, Sambol saw the frail being with its two swords, still running amock. The whole defense department was pitted against it. It seemed the short monster had escaped somehow, or vanished into thin air.

Across the skin of the being were various scratches, cuts and bruises- but nothing enough to shut it down permanently. In a world of kill or be killed, Sambol was not so fond of the latter. Recovering from the battle with his extra provisions, he chewed on an energy rich twig- that would boost his metabolism and gulped down from his bottle of water.

Ready for action, Sambol and Jonard both marched towards the opponent. During the ensuing battle, Sambol heard Nartejj order a team combination. It seemed he was injured; currently he was the one fighting the being. Well he was fighting the being which had four arms and used two to wield one sword, so he was pitted against one sword- but even that was too strong for Nartejj. The other was to keep anyone else from interfering. But Sambol was not one to back down.

It seemed Sambol's sword had a rhythm of its own, it moved up to the left then up to the right, horizontally left, horizontally right and then a straight

TOWN OF DUDLEY SIXTH

jab, which transformed into a horizontal slash followed by a vertical one. As he attacked the nuisance with all he had. In the time he had distracted the other sword, Kilurb used his ring sword to hack at the being's throat. Zain fired a poisoned arrow straight at the fresh cut. Gerath jabbed his halberd at the being's chest, while Raza whacked it in the stomach. This caused the monster to spit blood. In that short window, James threw a few chemical explosives into the being's mouth. That stopped it from moving and doing any more damage. Once the realization set in, that the battle was finally over they began to clean up.

They tied up the mutants and took them for inspection. While they moved the mutants, Gerath saw a paper fall from the robes one of the mutants was wearing.

He hid it in his pocket and asked Sambol to come with him to rest. When they were out of view, Gerath told Sambol about the piece of paper, mentioning it was his right to read it first. Sambol opened it and began to read, "The four Class A mutants are ordered to attack from the West using low concentrated mutating agents, while a full-fledged army is to take them on from the East using highly concentrated mutating agents. Our insider will weaken both sides of the wall simultaneously from the inside and outside. A few mutants should be able to push their way through. Note that this is a direct order from the Emperor of the wasteland; Zarrar."

He dropped the paper. Could the mysterious person he saw on his way home be the insider? But he didn't have time to think over the details. The Eastern border was where Engelia was stationed and the side where his home was located. The colour drained from

TOWN OF DUDLEY SIXTH

Sambol's face. He didn't utter a sound. Trembling with fear for his loved ones, Sambol ran towards the Head Commander, and gave him the note.

After reading the contents, Nartejj became red with anger and pale with fear. He called for all the forces to be rallied and prepare for war. His instructions were simple: half the forces, with Sambol, were to go outside the city and attack the enemy from the rear. Nartejj would take the other half to meet them in combat from the front. This was what he had feared for years. Just when his hopes became lifted, hell broke loose on his beloved city.

Nartejj took his half on horses, to confront the enemy. Sambol's group left the city, once the tall gates opened with the sound of gears rotating. They could have gone from the broken part of the wall, but they wanted to go with pride. Unaware of what lay beyond, the forces cried a battle cry and the thunderous sound of footsteps echoed as they entered Tenebris Mundo. The prolonged war was finally coming to an end, but at what cost?

TOWN OF DUDLEY SIXTH

Sword of Hope

Have you ever seen a day or a night that fails to come?

Whenever the darkness overwhelms the light, it is only overwhelmed by light again.

Does history not repeat all those cruel crude things?
Sometimes it does so but with just a little twist.

Victory in the battle between both sides,
Lives not long enough to get old.

The battle is swept in the tides of an everlasting war,
A war waged by the illuminating light against the destructive dark.

Many fall prey to the reapers call; others live only far too long,
For a war that began before all time, it can only end when it comes to an end.

Hidden in the dark, is always a pocket of light,
What hope can it have to shine once more?

Wedged between the abyss of darkness,
With its dim light, for what purpose does it live to serve?

Alas, neither does the dark become the light, nor does the light become the dark,
One can only push the other away, only to be pushed back in due time.

Never make the mistake to think that the dark will never come,
It only awaits the right chance, for the enemy is not so far gone.

TOWN OF DUDLEY SIXTH

Hope is all that the marchers have,
A march of the light headed into the depths of the dark.

For when even the darkest of pits is flooded by light,
Some chance there is that the truth shall come forth.

What truth may come forth, might you ask?
The truth is that the light cannot destroy the dark, nor can the dark destroy the light.

All life gives, is a cycle of vengeance and hatred,
Care to find the goodness within?

Both sides have their monsters within,
Do you not see how they take life from them all?

Yet claim they do that they are fighting for good,
Fighting is fighting, and fighting is never good.

TOWN OF DUDLEY SIXTH

Ranking of Both Departments

Defence Department
- Rookie
- Amateur
- Soldier
- Tudor
- Special Tudor
- Agent
- Chief Agent
- Heavenly Guardian
- Field Soldier
- Secondary Tower Militia
- Primary Tower Militia
- Gate Keeper
- Lead Gate Keeper
- Paradox Soldier
- Paradox Commander
- Rookie Samurai (optional for those who want to learn the way of the sword)
- Professional Samurai (optional for those who want to learn the way of the sword)
- Warrior
- Knight
- Legendary Knight
- Elite Knight
- Core Commander
- Head Commander

TOWN OF DUDLEY SIXTH

Scavenging Department

- Rookie
- Amateur
- Tudor
- Scavenger
- Gate Keeper
- Lead Gate Keeper
- Talented Scavenger
- Professional Scavenger
- Exotic Scavenger
- Field Spy (optional for those who want to go deep in unknown territory)
- Agent Spy (optional for those who want to go deep in unknown territory)
- Defenders
- Rare Defenders
- Uncommon Guardian
- Heavenly Guardian
- Engineer
- Material Specialist Engineer
- Mechanical Engineer
- Commander of Engineers
- Scavenging Knight
- Legendary Scavenging Knight
- Core Commander
- Head Commander

Note: Some Ranks can be skipped. Also one can pledge to be committed to a certain rank (i.e. for the rest of the term stay at the given rank, but one can only commit to a rank higher than Agent for Soldiers and Gate Keeper for Scavengers)

TOWN OF DUDLEY SIXTH